Wonderful Things

Written by Dana Meachen Rau
Illustrated by Viki Woodworth

Reading Advisers:

Gail Saunders-Smith, Ph.D., Reading Specialist

Dr. Linda D. Labbo, Department of Reading Education,
College of Education, The University of Georgia

LEVEL C

A COMPASS POINT
EARLY READER

For Chris

A Note to Parents

As you share this book with your child, you are showing your new reader what reading looks like and sounds like. You can read to your child anywhere—in a special area in your home, at the library, on the bus, or in the car. Your child will associate reading with the pleasure of being with you.

This book will introduce your young reader to many of the basic concepts, skills, and vocabulary necessary for successful reading. Talk through the details in each picture before you read. Then read the book to your child. As you read, point to each word, stopping to talk about what the words mean and the pictures show. Your child will begin to link the sounds of the letters with the look of the words that you and he or she read.

After your child is familiar with the story, let him or her read the story alone. Be careful to let the young reader make mistakes and correct them on his or her own. Be sure to praise the young reader's abilities. And, above all, have fun.

Gail Saunders-Smith, Ph.D.
Reading Specialist

Compass Point Books
3722 West 50th Street, #115
Minneapolis, MN 55410

Visit Compass Point Books on the Internet at *www.compasspointbooks.com* or e-mail your request to *custserv@compasspointbooks.com*

Library of Congress Cataloging-in-Publication Data

Rau, Dana Meachen, 1971–
   Wonderful things / by Dana Meachen Rau ; illustrated by Viki Woodworth.
      p. cm. — (Compass Point early reader)
   Summary: A boy compares himself to his friend Maria, who can make beautiful things, but Maria reminds him that he has talents she lacks.
   ISBN 0-7565-0075-3
      [1. Individuality—Fiction.] I. Woodworth, Viki, ill. II. Title. III. Series.
   PZ7.R193975 Wo 2001
   [E]—dc21
                                            00-011847

Maria can make butterflies
out of paper.

I just make a mess.

5

She can make puppets
out of bags.

I just make a mess.

She can make castles
out of boxes.

I just make a mess.

"You make wonderful

things," I say to Maria.

"I just make a mess."

"But I can't run races
like you can," Maria says.

"I can't play ball

like you can," Maria says.

"I can't make new friends
like you can," Maria says.

Then we get an idea!

Maria can make

wonderful things.

I can do wonderful things.

27

We make a great team!

More Fun with Wonderful Things!

Together, you and your child can host a backyard Olympics. This activity can be large-scale or small-scale, and provides an opportunity to show your child how to plan, stay organized, and have fun in the process!

- Collect paper, markers, glue, glitter, and other supplies so that you and your child can make awards, decorations, and signs.

- Help your child invite family and friends and organize games and sports.

- Set up activities together, such as a sack race, water balloon toss, obstacle course, or anything fun you and your child can think of.

- Shop together with a list of snacks needed. Make snacks before guests arrive.

- Have a great time and be sure everyone gets a prize!

Word List

(In this book: 39 words)

a	great	puppets
an	I	races
bags	idea	run
ball	just	say
boxes	like	says
but	make	she
butterflies	Maria	team
can	mess	then
can't	new	things
castles	of	to
do	out	we
friends	paper	wonderful
get	play	you

About the Author

Dana Meachen Rau is an author of more than fifty books for children. She loves making things, and her office in Farmington, Connecticut, is filled with her many projects. She keeps a big box of stuff in her closet with wrapping paper, sticks, feathers, juice lids, sandpaper, old magazines, crayons, paint, and yarn in it. Then, when she feels like making something, she has everything she needs. She loves to make goldfish out of colored paper and elephant trunks out of paper towel rolls. Her son, Charlie, is just finding out how fun and messy it is to color with markers.

About the Illustrator

Viki Woodworth lives in Seattle, Washington, with her husband and two teenage daughters. She has illustrated and written many books for children. The illustrations for this book were done with ink and watercolor on special paper.

32